How this collection works

This collection of traditional tales offers four well-loved stories from around the world for you and your child to enjoy together: *The Foolish Fox, Tom, Dad and Colin, Jack and the Beanstalk* and *The Magic Paintbrush*. They are based on traditional stories that your child may already be familiar with, but have been written so that your child can read them for themselves. They are carefully levelled and in line with your child's phonics learning at school. In addition, each story is accompanied by an optional extended story text for parents to read aloud to their child, to offer the richness that the original story language provides.

How to use this book

Find a time to read with your child when they are happy to concentrate for about 10–15 minutes. Reading with your child should be a shared and enjoyable experience. Choose one or two stories for each session, so they don't get too tired.

Please read the tips on the next page of this collection, as they offer suggestions and ideas for how to get the most out of this story collection.

Enjoy sharing the stories!

Tips for reading the stories together

Step 1 – Before you begin, ask your child to read the title of the story. Talk about what the story might be about. To set the scene of the story, read the extended story text available before each story. This will provide the rich story language of the original story and will familiarise the child with the plot and the characters before they read the story for themselves. Talk about the story and what your child liked and didn't like.

Step 2 – Now encourage your child to read the illustrated story to you. Talk about the pictures as you read. Your child will be able to read most of the words in the story, but if they struggle with a word, remind them to say the sounds in the word from left to right and then blend the sounds together to read the whole word, e.g. f-ar-m, farm. If they come across a tricky word that they cannot sound out, simply read the word to the child, e.g. said, like, were.

Step 3 – After you have read the story, talk about what happened. How are all the different characters feeling at the end of the story? Encourage your child to use the story map that follows each story to retell the story to you in their own words. It's a fun way of helping them to understand the story and to learn to tell stories in their own way.

Contents

OXFORD
UNIVERSITY PRESS

The Foolish Fox

Once upon a time there was a fox who owned a beautiful farm. But he wasn't interested in looking after it himself.

"What I need," he said, "is someone to do all the hard work for me."

And as luck would have it, who should pass by that very morning but a group of sheep, looking for work.

"We will look after your farm for you," said the sheep in charge. "All we ask in return," said the sheep, "is that you let us keep half of the food we grow."

Then the sheep asked the fox, "Can we keep the top part of the crops or the bottom part?"

"The top part," said the fox.

The sheep agreed and set to work. The foolish fox couldn't believe his luck!

First they ploughed the fields and sowed some seeds. Then they watered and weeded and the corn seeds began to grow.

But while the sheep worked hard, the foolish fox just relaxed and did what he liked.

Months went by, and the crops grew until the leaves were straight and tall and the corn was ripe and just ready for eating. The sheep harvested the corn crop and sorted it into tops and bottoms. Then they took the bottom of the corn crop to the fox.

When the fox saw the pile of roots, he was very cross.

"I can't eat these!" he said. Then when he saw the pile of juicy ripe corn for the sheep, he realised he had been tricked.

The fox thought for a while and then he spoke to the sheep.

"Next time, you must keep the bottom of the crops and I will keep the tops," said the fox.

The sheep agreed and set to work. The foolish fox couldn't believe his luck!

First they ploughed the fields and sowed some seeds. Then they watered and weeded and the turnip seeds began to grow. But while the sheep worked hard, the foolish fox just relaxed and did what he liked.

Months went by, and the crops grew until the leaves were bushy and green and the turnips were ripe. Then the sheep harvested the turnips and sorted them into tops and bottoms.

Then they took the top of the turnip crop to the fox. When the fox saw the pile of leaves he had been given, he was very cross.

"I can't eat these!" he said.

Then when he saw the pile of ripe turnips for the sheep, he realised he had been tricked AGAIN!

The fox was so cross with himself for being so foolish, he sent the sheep on their way. And from that day to this, he has farmed his land himself.

The Foolish Fox

Written by Alison Hawes

Illustrated by Matte Stephens

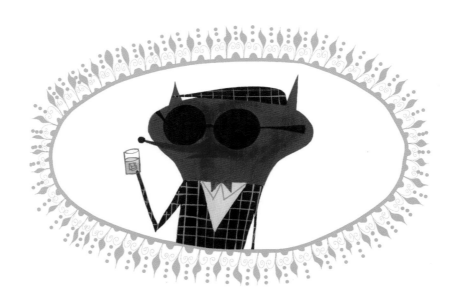

Fox

Sheep

Fox had a farm but he
did not like farming.

So he said to some sheep, "Farm my land for me, and you can keep some of the food."

The sheep said, "Can we keep the *top* part of the food or the *bottom* part?" "The top part," said Fox.

So the sheep put corn seeds in the soil.

When the corn was high,
the sheep cut it down.

Then they took the corn
roots to Fox.

"This is not food!" said Fox.
Fox was cross. It had been a trick!

15

Fox said, "Next year, you must keep the *bottom* part of the food."

So the sheep put turnip seeds in the soil.

When the turnips were big,
the sheep dug them up.

They took the turnip tops to Fox.

"This is not food!" said Fox.
Fox was cross. It had been a trick!

So now, Fox farms his land himself!

Once upon a time...

The end.

Tom, Dad and Colin Extended Story

There was once a boy called Tom who lived with his dad in a small village. One day, Tom and Dad decided to go to market. They had baskets full of apples to sell. They loaded the apples onto their donkey, Colin. Then Dad climbed onto Colin's back and Tom marched happily ahead.

The day was hot, the road was hard and the market was a long way off. He walked more and more slowly.

A passer-by called out to Dad.

"Why are you being so mean?" he shouted. "You should let your son ride. He's only a boy."

Dad did as he was told. He jumped off Colin and let Tom ride instead. They carried on down the long, dusty road.

The sun was beating down and soon Dad felt very tired. He could hardly put one foot in front of the other.

A man with a horse saw Dad trudging along.

"You lazy boy!" he said to Tom. "You shouldn't let your dad walk on such a hot day. Move along so he can ride too."

Tom did as he was told. Dad climbed up onto Colin's back and sat in front of Tom. Colin staggered along the road, sagging under the weight of Tom, Dad and the apples.

They passed an old man sitting on a bench with his dog.

"You're cruel!" he complained to Tom and Dad. "Your poor donkey needs a rest. You should be carrying him."

Tom and Dad did what they were told. They got down from Colin and Colin got on their backs instead.

Off they went, along the hot, dusty road to market. Colin and the apples were very heavy and soon Tom and Dad's feet began to hurt again. So did their arms and their backs.

When they reached the town all the children saw this strange sight and began to laugh at them. Tom and Dad felt foolish and wished they'd stayed at home. Colin felt foolish too.

Tom and Dad plodded along, under the weight of Colin and the apples. They didn't see the pond ahead. Before they knew what was happening – splash! They'd all fallen in!

Tom and Dad and Colin sat in the pond, with the apples bobbing around them. They were wet and fed up.

"We were foolish," sighed Tom.

"You're right," agreed Dad. "We should have thought for ourselves instead of listening to everyone else."

Tom, Dad and Colin

Written by Jan Burchett and Sara Vogler

Illustrated by Tony Ross

Tom set off for town, with his dad on Colin's back.

Little Town 8

27

Plod, plod, plod went Tom's feet
down the long, hard road.

A man went up to Dad.
"Let him get on," he said.

So Dad got down from Colin's back.
Tom got on Colin.

Plod, plod, plod went Dad's
feet down the long, hard road.

A man ran up to Tom.
"Let him get on too," he said.

So Dad got on Colin.

Clop, clop, clop went
Colin's feet down
the long, hard road.

Little Town 3

33

A man sat on a bench.
"Let him have a rest," he said
to Tom and Dad.

So they got down from Colin's back. Colin got on Tom and Dad.

Plod, plod, plod they went down the long, hard road to town.

Little Town 1

When they got to town,
lots of children were
looking at them.

Little
Town

Tom and Dad felt foolish.

Tom and Dad did
not see the pond.

Splash!

They all fell in.

Tom and Dad were fed up.
Now they were wet...

...and so was Colin!

Once upon a time...

The end.

Jack and the Beanstalk `Extended Story`

Once upon a time, there was a boy called Jack. He lived with his mother in a cottage. Every day, Jack's mother milked their cow, and Jack took a jug of milk to sell at the market. But one day, there was no milk!

"If we have no milk to sell, we will have no money," said Jack's mother. "Let's sell the cow."

On the way to market, Jack met an old man.

"Will you sell me your cow? I will pay five beans for her," he said.

So Jack sold the cow. But when his mother saw the five beans, she was angry.

"What use are beans?" she cried. And she threw them on the ground!

In the morning, Jack saw an enormous beanstalk. It was as high as the sky! He climbed up it. At the very top, there stood a giantess!

"You look hungry," she said to Jack. "I'll bake you some bread."

But then the ground began to shake, and Jack heard a voice like the north wind:

"Fee-fi-fo-fum ..."

"It's the giant! Quick, hide in that chest!" whispered the giantess.

The giant stamped in and sat down at the table. He started to count his gold coins. After a while, the giant began to snore. Jack crept out of the chest, grabbed three gold coins, and ran down the beanstalk.

The next day, Jack climbed the beanstalk again. There, at the top, was the giantess!

"You look hungry," she said. "I'll make a pie."

But then the ground began to shake, and Jack heard a voice like thunder:

"Fee-fi-fo-fum ..."

"Quick, hide in that pot!" said the giantess.

The giant sat down. He picked up his hen, and she laid two golden eggs! After a while, the giant began to snore. Jack crept out, grabbed the hen, and ran home.

The next day, Jack climbed the beanstalk again. And there was the giantess!

"You look hungry," she said. "I'll bake a cake."

But then the ground began to shake, and Jack heard a voice like a hurricane:

"Fee-fi-fo-fum ..."

"Quick, hide in that box!" said the giantess.

The giant stamped in, and sat down at the table. He picked up his golden harp, and started to play. After a while, he began to snore. Jack crept out of the box and grabbed the harp. But his hand touched one of the strings – *plink!* – and the giant woke up!

He roared, and chased Jack down the beanstalk! But Jack's mother stood at the bottom with an axe. As soon as Jack was on the ground, she chopped the beanstalk down!

So that was the end of the beanstalk ... and the giant! And Jack and his mother lived happily ever after.

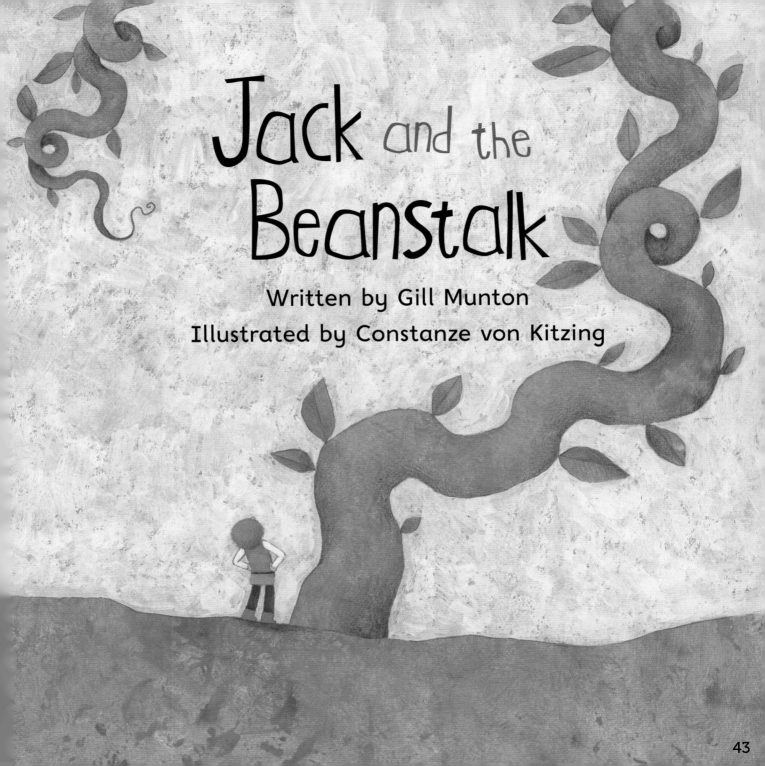

Jack and the Beanstalk

Written by Gill Munton

Illustrated by Constanze von Kitzing

Jack and his mum had a cow.
Each day, Jack took a jug of the cow's milk to market.

One day, there was no milk!
"Let's sell the cow," said Jack's mum.
"Then we can get some food."

Jack and the cow set off to market.
They met an old man.

"Will you sell me your cow?" he asked. "I'll pay you five beans."

"All right," said Jack.

When he got home, Jack's mum threw the beans away!
"Oh, Jack!" she cried. "What use are beans?"

The next day, one bean had grown into a huge beanstalk! Jack climbed up it.

49

At the top, he saw a giantess!
"You look hungry," she said. "I will
bake some bread."

Clink!

The giant had lots of gold coins.
He started to count them.

The giant fell asleep.

Zzz

Jack crept out of the chest and grabbed three gold coins. Then he ran home.

The next day, Jack climbed up the
beanstalk again.
"You look hungry!" said the giantess.
"I will cook a pie."

But then...

Fee-fi-fo-fum!
Can I smell a boy?

"It's the giant! Quick, hide!"
said the giantess.

Squawk!

The giant had a hen.
She laid golden eggs!

56

The giant
fell asleep.

Jack crept out
of the pot and
grabbed the hen.
Then he ran home.

The next day, Jack climbed up
the beanstalk for the third time.

"You look hungry!"
said the giantess.
"I will make a cake."

But then...

Fee-fi-fo-fum!
Can I smell a boy?

"It's the giant! Quick, hide!" said the giantess.

59

Plink!

The giant had a golden harp.
He started to play it.

Then he fell asleep.

Jack crept out of the box and grabbed the harp.

Zzz

Plink!

61

The giant woke up!
"Come back!" he shouted.

Jack ran down the beanstalk.
The giant followed him!

But Jack's mum stood at the bottom with an axe! She chopped down the beanstalk.

So that was the end of the beanstalk, and Jack and his mum had all the food they needed!

Once upon a time...

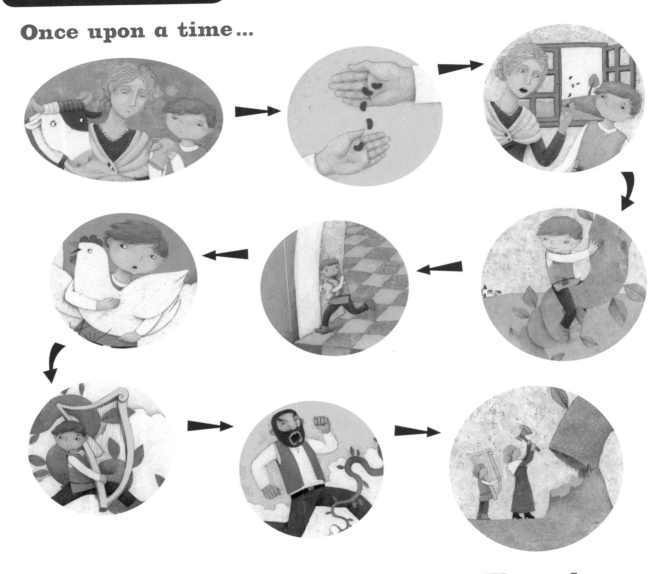

The end.

The Magic Paintbrush Extended Story

Long ago in a tiny village, there lived a young man called Ho. Every day, Ho worked hard, tending the rich farmer's cattle.

The mean farmer paid so little for his work that Ho could only buy stale bread to eat. Day by day, Ho became thinner.

One evening, a very thin old man limped up the lane.

"Oh dear," thought Ho. "How hungry he looks." He gave the man his bread.

The man thanked Ho and said, "My friend, because you are kind, take this. It's a very special paintbrush. Use it kindly."

Ho gathered plants and berries. In his hut, he mixed paints of many colours.

Ho dipped the paintbrush in yellow and painted a bale of hay. Whoosh! The hay became real! "It's a magic paintbrush!" gasped Ho.

The hot sun had dried up the earth. There was no water to drink. Ho dipped the paintbrush in blue and painted a stream. Whoosh! The stream became real! People filled their buckets with the fresh cool water.

Ho went to the farm. The farmer was having a feast while his workers and their children went hungry. "It's not fair," thought Ho.

Ho started to paint and the magic did its work. Soon, there was food for everyone!

Kind Ho used the paintbrush to help the poor. He painted a wheel, a bucket and some clothes.

"Thank you, Ho!" said the people.

But the wicked rich farmer wanted the magic paintbrush for himself. "To jail with Ho!" he said.

"The paintbrush will make me the richest man on earth," thought the greedy farmer. He painted gold. But nothing happened.

The farmer shouted for Ho to be brought to him. "Make the magic work!" he yelled. "Paint me a mountain of gold."

Ho painted a mountain of gold on an island in the middle of a blue sea. It became real.

The farmer said angrily, "How can I get the gold now? I can't swim! Do something!"

"I will paint you a ship," said Ho. He painted a ship in the sea.

The farmer sailed off towards the island. He laughed as the ship bobbed on the waves. "When I get back with my gold, you will paint everything I desire!" called the farmer.

But Ho was too busy painting to hear him. Ho painted a gale. The raging storm carried the wicked farmer far, far away.

Back at the farm, all the good people were pleased to hear what had happened. Ho painted only important things for the kind people of this world, and the greedy farmer was never seen again.

The Magic Paintbrush

Written by Liz Miles

Illustrated by Meilo So

Every day, Ho looked
after a rich farmer's
cattle. He took hay
to the field.

The farmer did not pay him much. Ho had
only dry bread to eat.

One day a very thin, old man came up the lane. He looked hungry. Ho gave his bread to the man.

Take this.

"Thank you," said the man. He gave Ho a gift. It was a golden paintbrush.

73

Ho made paints
from plants, berries
and mud.

"What shall I paint?" thought Ho. He began to paint some hay. The hay became real!

This is a magic paintbrush!

The sun was hot. The
stream was dry. So Ho
painted a blue stream.

The stream became
real! Now the
people and the
animals had
water to drink.

The rich farmer had lots of food to eat.
But the children and workers were hungry.

Ho painted lots
of food. It
became real!

Ho painted lots of things for people.
They all became real. He painted ...

a wheel ...

a bucket ...

and some clothes.

The rich farmer
wanted the magic
paintbrush. He put
Ho in jail and took
the brush.

The farmer was greedy. He painted gold. But the gold did not become real.

"Oi, you! The paintbrush does not work for me. Paint me a mountain of gold!" ordered the farmer.

Ho painted the mountain of gold. He painted a blue sea all around it. The gold and the sea became real.

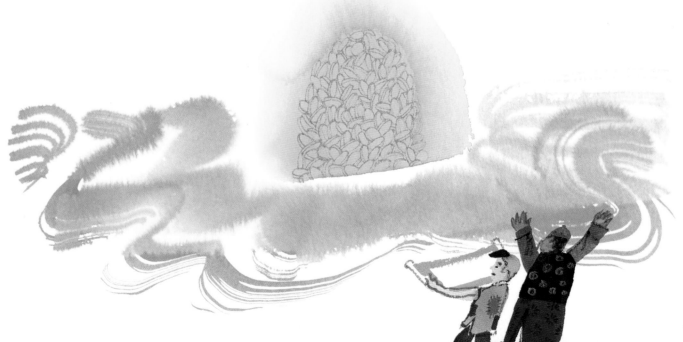

The farmer was angry.
"I cannot swim! Why did you paint
the sea?" he shouted.

"I will paint a ship for you,"
said Ho. The ship became real.

The farmer set off in the ship.
"When I get back, you will paint everything
I want. The world will be mine!" he laughed.

But Ho painted a gale. The gale became real. It took the farmer, far, far away.

Ho returned to the farm. He painted things for those who were kind and good to others.

The rich farmer was never seen again.

Retell the story

Once upon a time...

The end.

Make up a new story!

Now have a go at making up your own story like the ones in this book. You can use the ideas here or make up your own!

1 **Start by choosing some characters.**

They could be from this book, or from your imagination.

2 **How will your story start?**

Are the characters going to go on an adventure or a journey? For example, what if Jack and Ho climbed another beanstalk and met a monster at the top?

❸ What happens next?

Do the characters get into danger, or
have another sort of problem?
For example, perhaps the monster
tries to chase them?

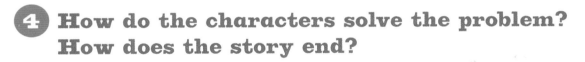

❹ How do the characters solve the problem?
How does the story end?

For example, does Ho paint something
to help them beat the monster?

Does Jack steal the
monster's treasure?

OXFORD
UNIVERSITY PRESS

Great Clarendon Street, Oxford, OX2 6DP, United Kingdom

Oxford University Press is a department of the University
of Oxford. It furthers the University's objective of excellence
in research, scholarship, and education by publishing worldwide.
Oxford is a registered trade mark of Oxford University Press
in the UK and in certain other countries

The Foolish Fox Text © Oxford University Press 2011
Illustrations © Matte Stephens 2011
Tom, Dad and Colin Text © Jan Burchett and Sara Vogler 2011
Illustrations © Tony Ross 2011
Jack and the Beanstalk Text © Oxford University Press 2011
Illustrations © Constanze von Kitzing 2011
The Magic Paintbrush Text © Oxford University Press 2011
Illustrations © Meilo So 2011

Extended story text for *The Foolish Fox* written by Alison Hawes
Extended story text for *Tom, Dad and Colin* written by Jan Burchett and
Sara Vogler
Extended story text for *Jack and the Beanstalk* written by Gill Munton
Extended story text for *The Magic Paintbrush* written by Liz Miles

The moral rights of the author have been asserted

The Foolish Fox, *Tom, Dad and Colin*, *Jack and the Beanstalk*, *The Magic
Paintbrush* first published in 2011

This Edition published in 2018

British Library Cataloguing in Publication Data
Data available

ISBN: 978-0-19-276519-2

10 9 8 7 6 5 4 3

Paper used in the production of this book is a natural, recyclable
product made from wood grown in sustainable forests. The
manufacturing process conforms to the environmental
regulations of the country of origin.

Printed in China

Acknowledgements

Series Advisor: Nikki Gamble